HUCKLEBERRY FINN

Samuel L. Clemens

ILLUSTRATED

NOW AGE BOOKS

Pendulum Press, Inc.

West Haven, Connecticut

ISBN 0-88301-093-3 Complete Set
      0-88301-098-4 This Volume

Library of Congress Catalog Card Number 73-75468

Published by
Pendulum Press, Inc.
An Academic Industries, Inc. Company
The Academic Building
Saw Mill Road
West Haven, Connecticut 06516

Printed in the United States of America

TO THE TEACHER

Pendulum Press is proud to offer the NOW AGE
ILLUSTRATED Series to schools throughout the country.
This completely new series has been prepared by the finest
artists and illustrators from around the world. The script
adaptations have been prepared by professional writers and
revised by qualified reading consultants.

Implicit in the development of the Series are several
assumptions. Within the limits of propriety, anything a
child reads and/or wants to read is *per se* an educational
tool. Educators have long recognized this and have clamored
for materials that incorporate this premise. The sustained
popularity of the illustrated format, for example, has been
documented, but it has not been fully utilized for educational purposes. Out of this realization, the NOW AGE
ILLUSTRATED Series evolved.

In the actual reading process, the illustrated panel
encourages and supports the student's desire to read printed
words. The combination of words and picture helps the
student to a greater understanding of the subject; and
understanding, that comes from reading, creates the desire
for more reading.

The final assumption is that reading as an end in itself is self-defeating. Children are motivated to read material that satisfies their quest for knowledge and understanding of their world. In this series, they are exposed to some of the greatest stories, authors, and characters in the English language. The Series will stimulate their desire to read the original edition when their reading skills are sufficiently developed. More importantly, reading books in the NOW AGE ILLUSTRATED Series will help students establish a mental "pegboard" of information — images, names, and concepts — to which they are exposed. Let's assume, for example, that a child sees a television commercial which features Huck Finn in some way. If he has read the NOW AGE Huck Finn, the TV reference has meaning for him which gives the child a surge of satisfaction and accomplishment.

After using the NOW AGE ILLUSTRATED editions, we know that you will share our enthusiasm about the series and its concept.

—The Editors

ABOUT THE AUTHOR

Samuel Langhorne Clemens was born in 1835 in Florida, Missouri. Later he and his family moved to Hannibal, Missouri. Since Hannibal was on the Mississippi River, one of Clemens' earliest ambitions was to be a cub pilot on a riverboat. In fact many of the adventures in *Huckleberry Finn,* probably are written from first-hand experience.

Mark Twain, the pen-name Clemens adopted, means two fathoms or safe water. Undoubtedly, he chose the name because of his love for life on the river, which is revealed in *Huckleberry Finn.* The novel becomes an embodiment of the dreams of American boyhood.

Twain had a gift for combining the humorous with the serious. His characters are real and believable, his settings are natural. He entertains while he instructs, a trait for which the ancients would praise him.

Other works by Samuel Clemens include: *Tom Sawyer, Pudd'nhead Wilson, Life on the Mississippi, The Prince and the Pauper, A Connecticut Yankee in King Arthur's Court,* and *The Celebrated Jumping Frog of Calaveras County* (his first).

Samuel Clemens
HUCKLEBERRY FINN

Adapted by
NAUNERLE FARR

a
VINCENT FAGO
production

Illustrated by
FRANCISCO REDONDO

Jim

Tom Sawyer

Huckleberry Finn

Widow Douglas

Pap

Huck Finn was a drop-out. He didn't like sleeping under a roof and wearing nice clothes and staying clean and doing things on time. He did like getting dirty and sleeping in the woods and playing hookey from school. So he ran away to float down the Mississippi River on a raft with his black friend, Jim, each looking for his own kind of freedom.

"There wasn't no home like a raft. Other places seem so crowded and stuffy. You might say the days swum by, they slid along so quiet and smooth and lovely. Nights we had the sky up there, all speckled with stars, and we used to lay on our backs and discuss about whether they was made or only just happened. Jim, he said they was made; I judged it would have took too long to make so many. Jim said the moon could 'a laid them. I didn't say nothing against it because I've seen a frog lay most as many."

When Pap was around, I mostly lived in the woods. But after he went away the Widow Douglas took me for her son and said she would civilize me. It was rough.

I had to wear nice clothes all the time.

Now Huck, dear, do try to stay clean and neat!

Yes'm.

I had to come to meals on time.

Can't I go a-swimming?

Not now... supper's ready.

But I couldn't eat till the Widow prayed some over the food.

On Sundays I had to wear shoes all day, and go to church!

Sit still, Huck!

I was only catching a fly.

Did you ever notice, if you're anywhere it won't do for you to scratch, you will itch all over?

Don't scratch in church, Huck!

But I itch in church!

Then her old maid sister, Miss Watson, came to live with her and she was worse.

Don't bend over like that, Huckleberry! Sit up straight!

Yes'm.

It was terrible living with them. But I stayed for one reason.

I tell you, Tom, I just can't stand it! I'm gonna run away.

But, Huck, we can't let you into my robber gang if you ain't somebody important. A robber has got to have family.

All right, Tom. I'll stick it out a while longer if you'll hurry and start the robber gang.

You bet! I'll get the boys together and we'll meet some night at midnight.

So one night after I heard the town clock strike twelve times, a twig snapped outside.

Mee-yow!

Mee-yow!

I climbed out of the window onto the shed and slid to the ground, and there was Tom.

Tom!

Come on. . . we'll go to our secret cave.

Now we'll start this band of robbers and call it Tom Sawyer's Gang. Everybody has got to take an oath!

What's the oath?

Every boy promises not to tell any secrets. If he does, he gets killed, and his family, too, and a curse put on him forever!

What about Huck? He's only got his old drunk father who ain't been seen for a year.

Everybody has to have somebody to kill.

Yes, or it wouldn't be fair and square to the others.

Everybody was bothered and I was almost ready to cry. Then I thought of a way.

How about Miss Watson, fellows? You can have her!

Oh, she'll do!

That's right!

Huck can come in!

Now what's this gang going to do?

Nothing, only robbery and murder and kidnapping and ambushes and such things. We'll be robbers and wear masks and stop wagons and stages.

We played robber now and then about a month, and then I quit. All the boys did. We hadn't robbed nobody, hadn't killed any people, but only just pretended. I couldn't see no reason in it. It was just boring. And there I was stuck with regular hours and going to school and Miss Watson.

One morning at breakfast I spilled the salt. I reached for some to throw over my shoulder to keep off bad luck, but Miss Watson was ahead of me.

Take your hands away, Huckleberry; what a mess you're making!

Now, sister. . . .

So I knew something bad was going to happen. And when I went outside, I saw somebody's footprints in the soft dirt.

Oh-oh! A cross in the left heel!

In a second I was running down the hill to Judge Thatcher's. He took care of my share of the robber money Tom and I found last year.

I don't see nobody yet!

I want to give you my six thousand dollars, Judge. . .all of it!

What can you mean, my boy?

Don't ask questions! Just take it. . .please!

Oho-o! I think I see.

Sign this paper, Huck, and I will keep the money safe for you.

And when I lit my candle and went up to my room that night, there sat Pap!

Pap! I thought it was you when I saw those footprints.

It's me all right!

And ain't you a sweet-smelling fellow! A bed and a mirror and a carpet on the floor. . .and your own father got to sleep with the hogs.

And they tell me you can read and write! Think you're better than your father now, don't you, because he can't!

Maybe I am, maybe I ain't.

And they say you're rich, too! That's why I come. You get me that money tomorrow!

I ain't got no money! Ask Judge Thatcher.

I'll ask him, all right! Him and the Widow, too. I'll show them they can't take my son and his money away from me. Now give me what you got on you.

I only got a dollar.

And drop that school, you hear? If I catch you going to school again, I'll whip you good!

He got to hanging around Widow's too much, and she threatened to make trouble. So one day in spring he waited for me.

Well, the old man went for Judge Thatcher in court to make him give up that money. The law-trial was a slow business. Meanwhile every time Pap got any money he got drunk and caused trouble and got jailed. This was fine with him. I hadn't wanted to go to school before, but I went now to spite Pap. He caught me a couple of times and whipped me.

I'll show them who's Huck Finn's boss! You come along with me, son.

He took me three miles up the river, where it was all heavy woods and no houses.

I got me an old cabin up here where nobody can find it.

There's a good lock on that door and I'm sleeping with the key under my head, so don't get no ideas about running away.

We lived on hunting and fishing. Pap kept me with him all the time.

It was kind of a good life and after a while I didn't want to go back to town.

Except every little while Pap went down to the store at the ferry and traded fish and game for whiskey, and brought it home and got drunk and beat me. And while he was gone, he locked me in. It was terrible lonesome. Once he was gone three days and I was scared I'd never get out.

Now you stay put while I'm gone.

I got no choice.

The window's not big enough for a dog to get through!

The chimney's too narrow.

I hunted the place over a hundred times. Finally I found something.

It's an old saw without any handle!

Finally, Pap got home with his jug, and started in to drink. I fell asleep.

I woke up later and Pap had gone kind of mad from the drink.

You're an Angel of Death, but you won't get me! I'll kill you!

I'll kill you dead!

Please, Pap... it's me — Huck!

Pretty soon he was all tired out....

Just let me rest a minute ...then I'll kill you.

Next time Pap went to town, I got busy.

I got to get away for sure.

I sawed out a part of a log. . . .

Made it! I'm free! I'll take Pap's gun and live in the woods.

I went along up the river bank, with one eye out for Pap and the other out for what the June floods might float down the river.

Hey — a lost canoe!

Now, I got a better idea. I'll go down river and camp.

With the canoe, I could carry supplies. On the way back to get them, I had an idea.

If I can fix it to look like robbers broke in and stole the stuff and killed me, folks will look for the robbers and won't bother no more about me!

I put the log pieces back and cleaned up the sawdust. Then I took the ax and smashed the door.

This sack of stones will look like they dragged my body to the river.

There goes my body!

It'll look like the robbers left this way with the supplies.

I wished Tom Sawyer was there. He'd have liked my escape plan.

I cleaned out the cabin like robbers would have done. . .everything that was worth a cent.

Bullets, coffee, sugar, fishlines, flour, blankets, matches. . . .

Then I pushed off.

I'll sail to Jackson's Island. Nobody ever goes there.

Jackson's Island was in the middle of the river, big and dark, like a steamboat without any lights.

It's mighty nice and peaceful out here.

It didn't take me long to get there. I ran the canoe in under the tree branches.

Nobody can see this from outside.

Then I stepped into the woods and laid down for a nap.

When I woke the next morning the sun was high. I felt lazy and comfortable. . .till I heard a noise.

Booooooom!

They're firing a cannon over the water, trying to make my body float!

The boat came in almost to shore. I laid behind a log and watched and listened.

There's Pap and Judge Thatcher and Tom Sawyer and Widow Douglas and everybody — and they're all talking about my murder!

The boat went all the way around the island and then back home, so I knowed I was all right.

Nobody else will come looking. Now I can make a nice camp.

For three days I did nothing but catch fish, eat berries, and explore. Then all of a sudden I bumped right into the ashes of a campfire.

I sneaked back on my tiptoes. I thought every tree stump was a man.

I'll hide my things and fix it to look like an old camp.

Then I climbed a tree. But after two hours. . . .

I can't live this-a-way. I'll have to find out who it is!

I slipped off towards where I'd seen the campfire. I went careful and slow. Sure enough there lay a man wrapped in a blanket.

It's gettin' gray daylight. . . soon he'll wake up.

Pretty soon he threw off the blanket and moved himself. It was Miss Watson's slave, Jim!

Hello, Jim! I bet I'm glad to see you!

It's Huck Finn's ghost!

Now I wasn't scared any longer. . .but Jim was!

I never harmed no ghosts! You get back in the river where you belong, and leave old Jim alone!

It didn't take long to make him believe I was alive. I was ever so glad to see Jim. I wasn't lonesome now.

But if it wasn't you killed, Huck, who was it?

Nobody! It was just a trick so people would leave me alone.

Jim had no supplies and no gun so he'd been eating berries and things. We caught a catfish and made a fire and had breakfast.

You must be almost starved, ain't you?

I bet I could eat a horse. I'm sure I could!

But what are you doing here, Jim?

You wouldn't tell on me, would you Huck?

Blamed if I would, Jim.

Well, Huck, I ...I ran off!

I heard Miss Watson say she could get $800 for me to sell me down the river. . .so I left.

Honest, I won't tell.

There was a high hill in the middle of the island with a big cave in it. Jim said it was going to rain, so we moved in.

When those little birds fly like that, it's a sure sign of rain.

You know signs for most everything, Jim.

It began to thunder and lightning, and rain like mad; and I never seen the wind blow so!

Look at those tree-tops a-plungin'!

Jim this is nice! Pass me another hunk of fish.

The river rose for ten or twelve days from the rain and melting snow. It was three feet on the low parts of the island, and we rowed all over. The sun was hot again but it was cool in the deep woods.

Look at the animals, Jim, keeping out of the flood!

We could have pets enough if we wanted them.

One night we caught a piece of a lumber raft.

Let's pull it in.

It's good and solid and level.

Another night, a frame house came floating down in the flood! We rowed out and tied up to it.

Looks like a man on the floor.

Hello, you!

He's dead. . . shot in the back. Come in, Huck, but don't look!

Guess we don't want these old cards and empty whiskey bottles!

No, but these old clothes might come in handy.

An old lantern, candles, sewing stuff, a fishline. . . .

It's good stuff, Jim.

We got home all safe, and the days went along, and the river went down. It began to get slow and dull.

I think I'll row over to town and see what's going on, Jim.

It's a good idea . . .but go in the dark, and be careful!

How about dressing like a girl in these old clothes?

How's this?

It's a fair fit. Nobody would know you. . . .

A disguise!

But quit pulling your dress up to get at your pants pockets.

I tied up at the bottom of town after dark. There was a light in a shack that was empty before, so I looked in the window.

I never saw her before so she won't know me.

Come in! Have a chair! What might your name be?

Sarah Williams, ma'm. I've walked a long way and I'm very tired.

My Mom's sick and out of money, and I've come to get help from my uncle. . . at the upper end of town.

You had best stay here all night. When my husband gets home, he'll go along with you.

He's gone to borrow a boat. He and a friend are going over to Jackson's Island tonight, to look for a runaway slave that's wanted for murder.

M-murder?

Outside, I was off in a hurry, back to the canoe.

Back on the island, I ran for the cave.

Git up, Jim! They're after us!

In half an hour everything we owned was loaded on our raft.

That's it, Jim.

We floated out and slipped along past the foot of the island, very quiet. . . .

With the first light of day we tied up in a hidden cove where we thought it was safe to fix the raft. Jim built a tent, and a raised floor, and a dirt fireplace.

This will keep our things dry, and us too!

And they won't get wet by the steamboat waves.

We traveled at night and hid in the daytime. The fifth night we passed St. Louis and it was like the whole world lit up.

I never believed there was so many people in St. Louis before!

And everybody's asleep but us.

When we get to Cairo we can sell the raft and get on a steamboat and go up the Ohio River into the states where there are no slaves.

Then I'll be a free man! I'll be shouting for joy and I'll say it's all because of Huck!

We judged three more nights would bring us to Cairo. The second night a fog began to come in.

We can't sail in this fog.

I'll take a rope to shore and tie us up.

But the raft was moving too fast because of the swift current. . . .

It's tore the tree out by the roots and it's gone!

I was scared sick. There wasn't no raft in sight. You couldn't see twenty yards.

It won't do to row, I'll run into something. I got to float. . . and listen.

I heard a whoop over this way!

No. . .it sounds like it's over there. . . .

I just give up then, I was too tired to bother no more.

I'll catch a little sleep.

When I woke up the fog was gone. Downstream I saw a black speck on the water.

Maybe that's the raft!

Jim!

You ain't drowned, Huck? It's too good to be true!

One thing worries me, Jim. . .suppose we passed Cairo in that heavy fog?

Worries me, too, Huck. At Cairo I'd be free.

But one minute past Cairo we're back in slave country again, all the way down the river!

So the next time we saw lights, I planned to row ashore and find out where we were.

That's Cairo ...I know it!

You stay out of sight till I find out for sure!

Right then along comes a boat with two men in it with guns.

We're looking for five slaves that run off last night. Any men on that raft?

One, my Pap.

I guess we'll go see for ourselves.

I wish you would. Pap's sick. . .and so is Mom and Mary Ann.

We'll be mighty thankful for help. Everybody else goes away when I ask them.

Well, that's mean! Odd, too.

Say, what's the matter with your father?

I was scared. It wasn't but a little way to the raft now.

It's the. . .a. . .well, it ain't anything much!

Darn it, I'll bet he's got the smallpox*! Keep away, boy! Why didn't you say so?

Everybody I've told they went away and left us!

We're right down sorry. . .but we don't want the smallpox! It wouldn't do any good to land here, it's only a woodyard.

You float along down twenty miles and you'll come to a town. Tell them your folks are down with chills and fever and they'll help.

* a very serious sickness that used to kill people

They rowed away in a hurry, and I went back to the raft.

Jim! He's not here!

Here I is, Huck. I was going to swim for it if they come. . .but you was too smart for 'em!

That night about ten we come in sight of the lights and I went off to ask about it.

We tied up for the day and hid the raft extra good. Jim spent the day fixing things in bundles, getting ready to quit rafting.

It makes me all over scared to be so close to freedom! That next town got to be Cairo!

Mister, is that town Cairo?

Cairo? No. Cairo's way back up the river.

I sure hated to tell Jim. I went back and we talked over what we could do.

We sure can't take the raft upstream.

I don't see no way but to start back in the canoe and take the chances.

We hid the raft, and slept all day in a cottonwood forest so as to be fresh for the work. And when we went back.

The canoe. . .it . . .it's gone!

We didn't say a word for a while. Then we talked it over.

I can't see nothing but to float along with the raft till we can find a canoe to buy.

We sure can't steal one. That might set people after us.

After dark, we floated out on the raft, hoping our spell of bad luck was over.

It's gettin' mighty dark and thick.

A steamboat's comin'. I'll light the lantern so she'll see us.

The steamboats never cared much for raftsmen. They'd try to see how close they could come without touching. This one headed right for us, big and scary over our heads.

There was a yell at us and a ringing of bells, and as Jim went into the water on one side and I on the other, she come smashing through the raft.

When I came to the top again, the boat was out of sight.

Jim!

Jim!

I didn't get any answer. I grabbed a floating log and swam for shore.

I guess it's a good two miles across, here.

It was so dark, I came across a big house before I saw it.

A lot of dogs jumped out barking. I knowed better than to move.

Who's that prowling around?

I'm George Jackson, sir. I fell off the steamboat.

Well, George, we've got you covered. Come in alone. Come mighty slow!

I took one slow step at a time. There wasn't a sound. I could hear my heart beat!

I put my head in and there they all was, looking at me, and me at them.

After I was fed, I went to bed with Buck. Next morning, darn it, I forgot my name. So I tried a trick.

My trick worked. I wrote my name down so I wouldn't forget it again.

These people, the Grangerfords, were a mighty nice family. They had a mighty nice house, and a hundred slaves.

Son, consider you have a home here, as long as you want it.

And Jack, here, will be your personal servant. Each of us has one.

I'm surely thankful to you!

But even Buck, the youngest, never went anywhere without his gun.

How come you always carry your gun, Buck?

That's because of the feud. I might want to kill a Shepherdson.

Feud. . . what's that?

Well, a man has a quarrel and kills another man; then that man's brother kills him; then the other brothers go for each other and cousins help too.

By and by everybody's killed off, but it's kind of slow. This one started thirty years ago. Three of my brothers has been killed.

Holy smoke, Buck!

Those Shepherdsons must be awful!

No, indeed! They're just as fine and brave as. . .as we are!

One day my boy Jack came up when I was alone.

If you will come into the swamp, I'll show you something mighty strange!

All right; go ahead. I'll follow.

He led me through the swamp to a bit of dry land in the middle, and there was a man.

Jim!

I'm surely glad to see you! I swum along behind you that night, but I didn't answer your yells for fear somebody would pick me up and take me into slavery again.

The slaves here been taking care of me, and helping me patch up the raft and fill it with supplies. Now we's ready to go again when you are!

That sure is good news, Jim.

When I woke the next day, that whole big place was still as a mouse . . .nobody around, inside or out, but my boy, Jack.

Where's everybody?

That feud thing started up again, and everybody took his gun and went to fight the Shepherdsons. They didn't want to mix you up in it.

I figured it was time for me to go. I went and found Jim and we pushed off for the big water as fast as we could.

Two or three days and nights passed, quiet and lovely. Days we found a place to hide. Nights, out we went on the river.

They was mighty nice people to me. If they're going to get killed, I'd sooner not know about it.

A raft's the place to live, Jim!

No place like it.

One morning at daybreak I found a canoe, and paddled up a creek to look for berries. All of a sudden a couple of men come running.

Save us, young fellow! There's men and dogs after us!

I took them aboard to where the raft was tied up. After breakfast, we all sat and talked. It come out that these men didn't know one another.

What got you into trouble?

I'd been selling something that takes the dirt off teeth. . . and it does, too. . . .

But it takes the enamel* off as well!

I was sliding out of town quick when I ran across you. What got the dogs on you?

I been running a little temperance revival*. Doing well, business growing all the time. . .till word got out I had my own bottle of whiskey that I drank when no one was around.

* the hard white covering that protects teeth from decay

* people who don't believe that people should drink whiskey

* Prince of France, and next King

The King and the Duke got pretty mad with each other over the difference in rank. It didn't take me long to figure they weren't no kings or dukes at all, but just fakes, but I never let on. Then they started asking us questions.

How come you don't sail in the daytime, and you hide up this way? Is he a runaway slave?

Goodness sakes, no!

When Pap died, all he left me was sixteen dollars and a piece of raft and his slave, Jim. I thought to take Jim and the raft down to Uncle Ben's farm south of New Orleans.

But people kept thinking Jim was a runaway, and trying to take him away from me. So we don't run daytimes no more.

Let me think. I'll make up a plan to fix it.

That night we floated down river, and tied up near a little town. Next day the Duke wanted to visit it.

I've got a plan. I must go to town to fix it.

You go along, too, Huck. We needs coffee.

What I'm after is a printing office.

The town looks empty.

Most everybody's gone out to the camp meeting.

Gosh sakes, can you work that?

Indeed, yes! Printing's my trade!

Can I get this horse ad printed?

Certainly, sir!

That'll be four dollars!

Looks good.

The Duke printed off two more jobs. . .and took the money. But the main job was one he printed for us.

$200 REWARD

SLAVE JIM

SLAVE JIM, RUN AWAY FROM ST. JACQUES PLANTATION NEAR NEW ORLEANS. REWARD AND EXPENSES FOR HIS RETURN.

Now we can run in the daytime. If anybody comes, we tie Jim up and say we caught him and are going for the reward.

We all said the duke was pretty smart. We could boom right along now if we wanted to.

But the Duke had more ideas.

Have you ever acted in plays King?

No!

The first good town we come to, we'll hire a hall, and put on Romeo and Juliet. This is how it goes. . . .

The Duke told us all about who Romeo and Juliet were, and that the King could be Juliet.

But ain't my bald head and white whiskers going to look funny on her?

These country people won't think of that. Besides, you'll be in costume.

Juliet's wearing her nightgown and her nightcap. It makes all the difference!

Well, the Duke and the King practiced, and we found a town, and the Duke hired the Courthouse and put up signs, and that night there was a big crowd to see the show.

The King and Duke floated down the river and planned more ways to get money from people.

I think they're going to rob somebody's house!

The very first chance, we clear out and leave them!

One day we tied up near a village and the King went ashore.

If I'm not back by noon, Duke, it's all right; you and Huck come along after me.

At noon we went along, and we found the King. . .so drunk he couldn't walk!

Why, you old fool. . . .

Let me alone, you!

I got away from them both and ran down the river road like a deer.

It'll be a long day before they see Jim and me again!

Now's our chance, Jim! Set her loose!

But Jim was gone!

I run this way and that in the woods, shouting.

Jim! Jim! Where are you?

Then I sat down and cried.

It's no use. . . old Jim's gone.

Have you seen a strange Negro around?

Yes, they've got him at the Phelps' place.

He's a runaway slave and they got him. Was you looking for him?

Huck knew it was the King who had turned Jim in with the fake ad about Jim being a runaway slave from New Orleans. He made up his mind to steal Jim from slavery.

I might as well go find the Phelps.

When I got near, a lot of dogs and people rushed out. . . .

It's you at last! . . .ain't it?

Dear, dear, I'm so glad to see you! Was the boat late? Tell me all about the family!

Well. . . yes'm. . . I. . . .

Children, come meet your cousin Tom. . .Tom Sawyer!

By jings, I almost fell through the ground to find out who I was! It was easy to be Tom Sawyer. . . .

At least as long as the real Tom didn't come along! And just then I heard a steamboat whistle.

Aunt Sally, could I take the wagon and go get my bags?

Of course, child!

If they were expecting Tom, he might be on this boat. Sure enough, I met him halfway.

Hold on, Tom!

You're. . .Huck Finn's ghost!

I ain't no ghost, Tom. . .Honest Injun!

Well. . .I. . . can't under-stand it!

Weren't you ever murdered at all?

No, it was a trick! But I'm in trouble now. . . .

So I told him the whole story.

. . . .and Jim is here, and I'm trying to steal him out of slavery.

I'll help you! I'll say I'm my brother, Sid, come to visit, too.

The Phelpses were very surprised.

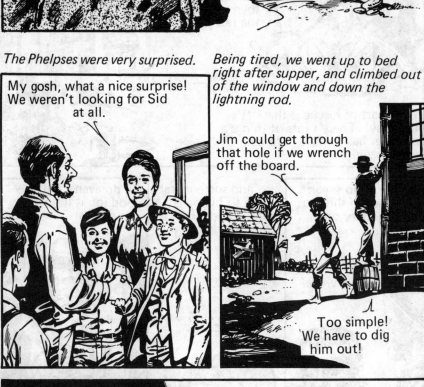

My gosh, what a nice surprise! We weren't looking for Sid at all.

Being tired, we went up to bed right after supper, and climbed out of the window and down the lightning rod.

Jim could get through that hole if we wrench off the board.

Too simple! We have to dig him out!

Even picks is going to take awhile!

Glory be!
It's Huck. . .
and Mr. Tom!

We can lift the
bed and slip off
that chain, and
then make for
the raft!

What sort of rescue is that? It's
too easy! There's lots of things a
prisoner has to have before he
can escape.

We've got to sneak
Jim a white shirt to
write a diary on. . . .

I can't
write.

. . . .and some metal
things to file pens
from. . .and a rope
ladder made from
sheets.

To do even a halfway
good job it'll take
some days!

I think Jim might have
liked it simple, and
him free. . .but he went
along with Tom's plans.

As time passed, Aunt Sally got mad and I got worried.

I've hunted high and low for your white shirt, Silas. What did you do with it? I want to know!

I think we ought to go ahead and set Jim free!

I'm writing a warning letter . . .so the escape won't go off too boring. How's this?

A DESPERATE GANG IS GOING TO STEAL YOUR RUNAWAY SLAVE TONIGHT!

UNKNOWN FRIEND

It worked real good. When we went out that night, fifteen farmers with guns were hiding around the yard.

We would have made it but Tom's pants caught on a splinter and snapped it.

We ran as fast as we could. The bullets fairly flew around us!

Who's that? Stop, or I'll shoot!

But we lost them, and made it to the raft.

Now, old Jim you're a free man again!

And it was done beautiful. . .all mixed up and wonderful!

The best of all is, I've got a bullet in my leg!

I don't move a step without a doctor for that leg.

No, that's crazy!

Huck can bring a doctor. I'll hide nearby while he's here.

Jim's right.

I got the doctor. Told him my brother got shot hunting. But back at the canoe there was a problem.

This canoe's not safe for two people. You wait here, boy.

But. . . .

I went home and worried and worried. Next morning we heard a loud group of people.

Let's hang the runaway!

Show the others what happens!

Sid! He's hurt!

No. . .he's a good man and should have kind treatment. Instead of escaping, he helped me care for the boy. Otherwise he could have gone from here, and been free.

Later, Tom came to.

I'm glad you're better. . .but Jim's locked up again.

They can't do that! He's a free man! Miss Watson died and set Jim free in her will.

Why didn't you say so?

I wanted to have a grand adventure rescuing him. Goodness alive, Aunt Polly!

I tried to hide.

All right, Tom now what?

That ain't Tom, it's Sid. . . .

That's Tom all right. The other one's Huck Finn. Come Huck!

They were the most mixed-upest-looking persons I ever seen.

When you wrote that Sid was here . . .and then never answered my questions. . .I came to find out for myself.

But I never got any letters!

I've. . .uh. . .been keeping them for you!

We had Jim out of the chains in no time, and when everybody heard how good he helped the doctor take care of Tom, they made a fuss over him. And we had him up to the sickroom and had a fine old talk.

Here $40, Jim, for being such a good prisoner. Now we three ought to sneak out of here some night, and get supplies, and go for adventures in Indian territory.

I ain't got no money to buy me an outfit. It's likely my Pap's been back before now, and got it all away from Judge Thatcher.

Your Pap ain't comin' back no more, Huck.

Remember the house we saw in the flood, and the dead man I didn't let you look at? That was your Pap.

There ain't nothing more to write about and I'm glad of it. If I'd knowed what trouble it was to make a book I wouldn't have done it. Now I got to leave ahead of the rest, because Aunt Sally, she plans to adopt me and civilize me, and I can't stand it.

I been there before!

THE END

WORDS TO KNOW

adopt	diary	raft
ambush	prowling	skiff
civilize		

QUESTIONS

1. Why did Huck take his money to the Judge for safe-keeping?

2. How did Huck get his pap to think he'd been murdered?

3. Why did Tom think Huck was a ghost when he first saw him?

4. Why wasn't Huck afraid when he found out that the other man on the island was Jim?

5. Why didn't Jim want Huck to look at the dead man in the floating house?

6. Why does Huck tell the men in the boat that Pap, Mom, and Mary Ann are sick?

7. What does this story about his family being sick tell you about Huck?

8. After Jim and Huck passed Cairo in the fog, why couldn't they turn the raft around and sail back?

9. What's a feud?

10. What is so silly about Tom's plan for Jim's escape?